Yellow Is My Color Star

Judy Horacek

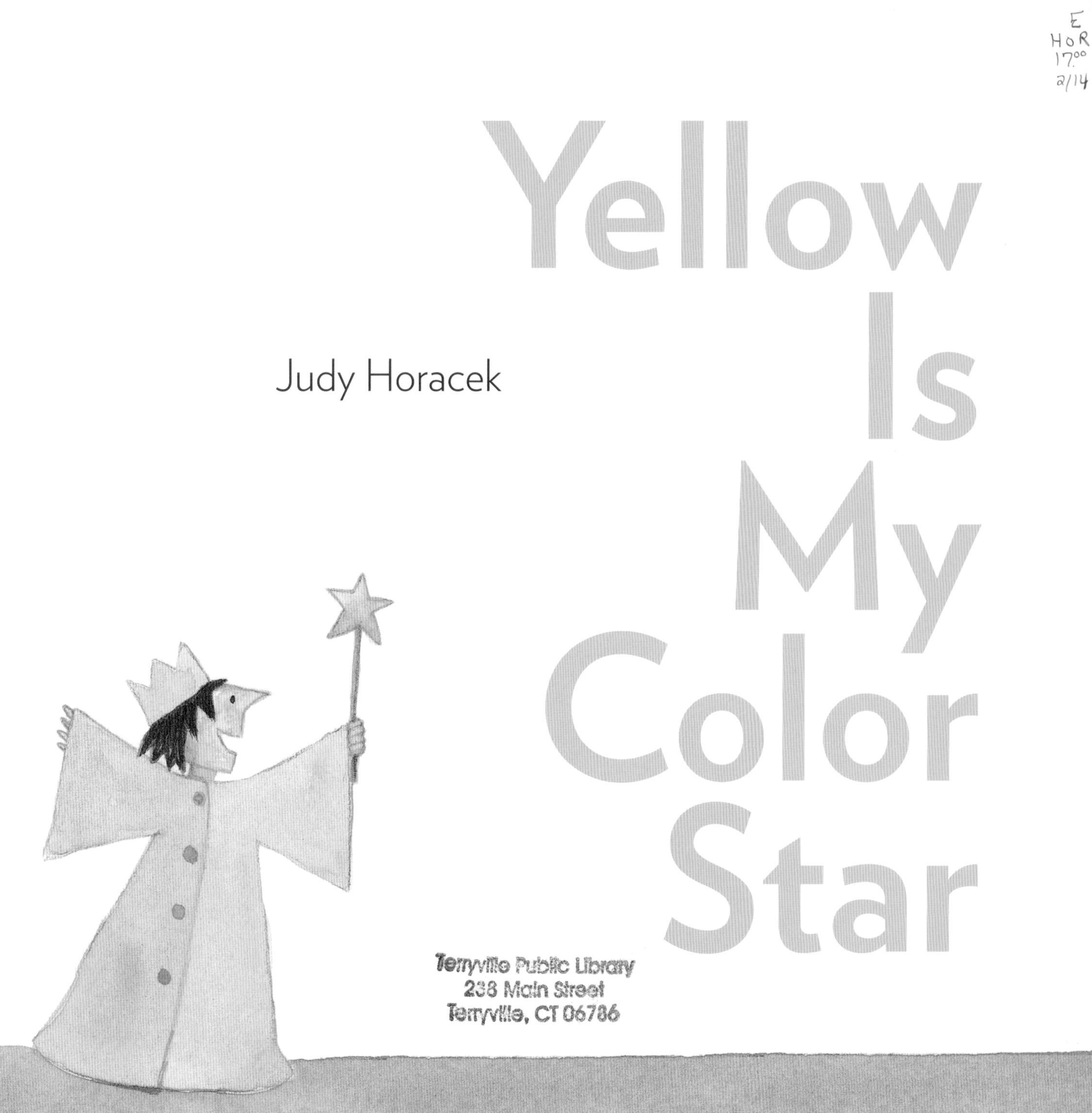

Beach Lane Books • New York London Toronto Sydney New Delhi

For Alice

BEACH LANE BOOKS
An imprint of Simon & Schuster Children's Publishing Division
1230 Avenue of the Americas, New York, New York 10020

Originally published in Australia in 2010 by the Penguin Group
First U.S. edition 2014

For information about special discounts for bulk purchases, please contact Simon & Schuster Special Sales
at 1-866-506-1949 or business@simonandschuster.com.
The Simon & Schuster Speakers Bureau can bring authors to your live event. For more information
or to book an event, contact the Simon & Schuster Speakers Bureau at
1-866-248-3049 or visit our website at www.simonspeakers.com.
Book design by Lauren Rille
The text for this book is set in Verlag.
The illustrations for this book are rendered in watercolor.
Manufactured in China
1013 SCP
10 9 8 7 6 5 4 3 2 1
Library of Congress Cataloging-in-Publication Data
Horacek, Judy.
Yellow is my color star / by Judy Horacek.—First edition.
p. cm.
Summary: Celebrates all the colors of the world, especially yellow.
ISBN 978-1-4424-9299-8 (hardcover)
ISBN 978-1-4424-9300-1 (eBook)
[1. Stories in rhyme. 2. Color—Fiction.] I. Title.
PZ8.3.H779Yel 2014
[E]—dc23
2013009628

Yellow is my favorite color.

I like red too,

and also blue.

Green is great.

And pink is fun.

But yellow is my number one.

To orange I say,
"Hip! Hip!"

To purple I say,
"Hooray!"

But yellow is the color
that brings sunshine to my day.

Which color do you love the most?

Which color could you eat on toast?

Which color is the queen for you?
Yellow, orange, red, or blue?

Purple? Green? Or maybe pink?

Which is the best?

What do *you* think?

Of all the colors that I see,

yellow is the one for me.

Yellow is the best by far.

It really is the color star!

Yes, yellow is my favorite color.

Which one is yours?

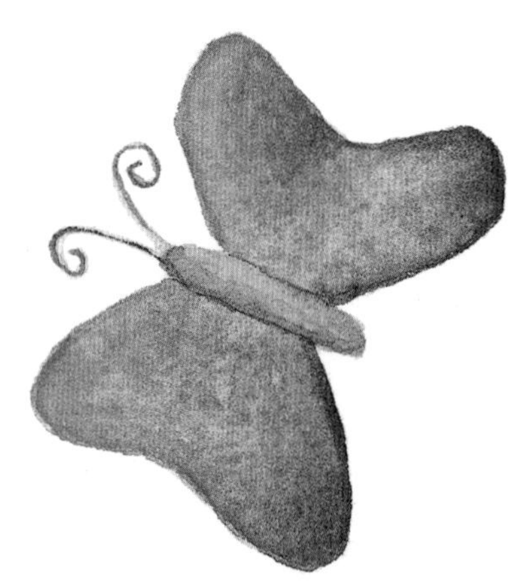

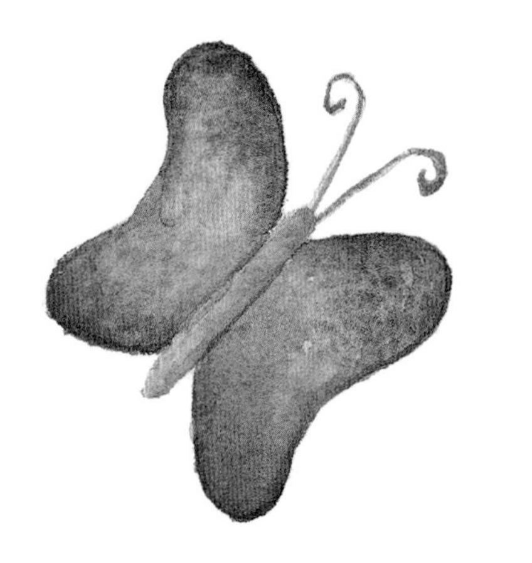

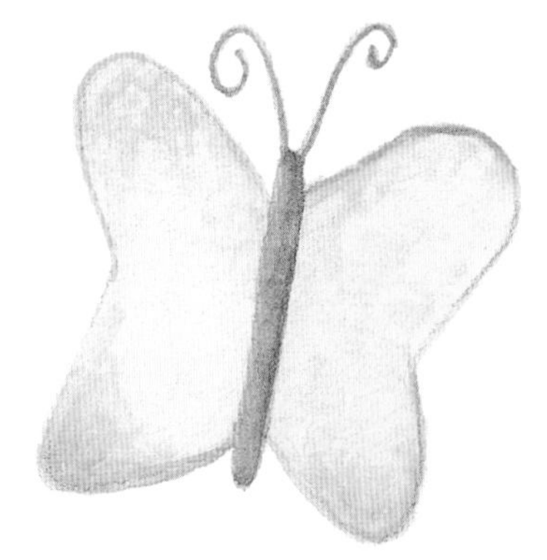